In memory of my grandmothers,
Margaret, Nora, and Catherine;
this is my song for you.
—Sacha

To Nana Vic and Nana Cav.
Thank you for keeping it real and making
the most beautiful splash in our lives.
—Josh

First published in the United States
by Sourcebooks in 2020
Text © 2018, 2020 by Sacha Cotter
Illustrations © 2018, 2020 by Josh Morgan
Cover and internal design © 2020 by Sourcebooks
Cover design © Travis Hasenour/Sourcebooks
Sourcebooks and the colophon are registered trademarks of Sourcebooks.
All rights reserved.
The illustrations in this book were created in Adobe Photoshop using digital
painting and found textures.
Published by Sourcebooks Jabberwocky, an imprint of Sourcebooks Kids
P.O. Box 4410, Naperville, Illinois 60567-4410
(630) 961-3900
sourcebookskids.com
Originally published as *The Bomb* in 2018 in New Zealand by Huia Press.
Library of Congress Cataloging-in-Publication Data is on file with the publisher.
Source of Production: Phoenix Color, Hagerstown, Maryland, USA
Date of Production: May 2020
Run Number: 5018962
Printed and bound in the United States of America.
PHC 10 9 8 7 6 5 4 3 2

CANNONBALL

Words by Sacha Cotter
Pictures by Josh Morgan

sourcebooks
jabberwocky

I'm always dreaming of pulling off
that *perfect* cannonball.
A booming one, a slapping one,
a splashing, dripping, soaking one!

$$V_2 = V_1 \frac{A_1}{A_2}$$

$$\rho \left(\frac{\partial v}{\partial t} + v \cdot \nabla v \right) = -\nabla p + \nabla \cdot \tau_D + f$$

Do an amazing cannonball around here,
and you'll be something all right.

SomeONE.

And *I've* been studying cannonballs *forever*!
Nan is an awesome teacher!
"What you wanna know, sunshine?

You wanna know about a staple?

How about a knee lock?

Bottle pop?

Coffin drop?

I know, I know, the MANU!
That's my favorite too.

Bend, bend. Now, lean back.
Don't forget the V.

You wanna land in a V.
That's it. Beautiful."

Everyone has their pre-jump rituals.
You've got your thinkers and your posers,

your dive-right-in-ers and your jokers.

Me, before *I* jump, I whisper,

"Hear my song, see my lines,
check my moves, they're so fine.
See me soar, see me fly,
see me swooping through the sky.
But watch out for my..."

Sometimes, I get the feeling that

I'm just not cut out for cannonballs.

Still, everyone has advice for me.

I listen to *everything* they say.
I do *everything* they tell me to do.

Once again, before I jump, I whisper.
But my voice is so quiet,
I'm not even sure it's there anymore.

"Hear my song, see my lines,
check my moves, they're so fine.
See me soar, see me fly,
see me swooping through the sky.
But watch out for my..."

"HURRY UP AND
JUMP ALREADY!"

...PLOP.

Even my belly flop fails to make a splash.

"Kid, it's time to accept what is TRUE!
Cannonballs aren't
for someone like YOU!"

But Nan, she's got other ideas.

"Come here, sunshine.
Of course cannonballs are for you!"

"Listen to *your* heart, to *your* mind,
to the pull that's inside. Do it *your* way."

"My way?"

"Yes, baby, *all* the way!"

Once I really listened,
it was easy to know
what to do.

"Nan! Nan! *I know!*

I'll take a flower for each ear,
let the breeze flow in my hair,

get a rainbow for some flair,
then go dancing through the air!

I will do it *my* way!"

"You'll shine like the stars, and you'll whirl like the wind!"

"And I'll do it my very own way!"

"You'll sing like the birds

and unfurl like a fern!"

"And I'll do it my own special way!"

This time, before I jump,
I shout to the water. I shout to the trees.
I shout to the clouds, and I shout to the leaves.
I shout to the sky, to the moon, to the sun.
I shout, I shout to everyone!
I shout out loud, because now I really see
that the voice I need to hear
is the voice that comes from me!

"Hear my song, see my lines,
check my moves, they're so fine.
See me soar, see me fly,
see me swooping through the sky.
But..."

"watch

out

for

my..."

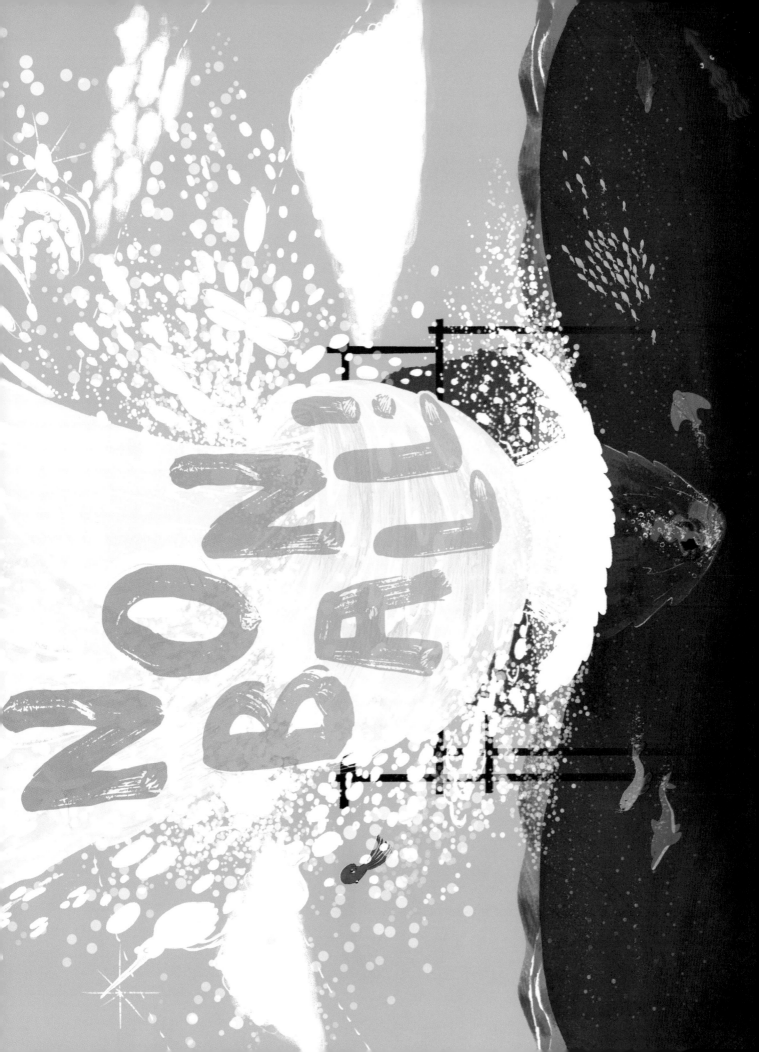

"Hear his song, see his lines,
check his moves, they're so fine.
See him soar, see him fly,
see him swooping through the sky...
HE'S THE BOMB!"

GLOSSARY

STAPLE DIVE: The diver jumps out, often forming a straight horizontal line, then folding in half, making a staple shape before hitting the water.

KNEE LOCK DIVE: The diver holds one knee to the chest and enters the water feetfirst.

BOTTLE POP DIVE: The diver holds an upside-down plastic bottle as they jump. After entering the water, the bottle shoots up like a rocket with the splash. The higher the better! Always bring the bottle with you when you leave the pool.

COFFIN DROP: The diver folds the arms over the chest and enters the water feet first.

MANU: A Māori word for bird. Divers often crouch down before take-off, then leap out and lean back. Most importantly, divers fold up their body to form a "V" shape before entering the water tailbone first.

PUKU: A Māori word for stomach or belly.